PEPIN'S TALE

ARIBOSLIA COMPANION

J. F. ROGERS

NOBLEBRIGHT
PUBLISHING

www.noblebrightpublishing.com

Pepin's Tale - An Ariboslia Companion
Revised Edition

Copyright © 2023 by J F Rogers
All rights reserved. No part of this book may be reproduced in any form
except by permission from the author.

This book is a work of fiction. Any resemblance to existing people or places
is purely coincidental.

ISBN: 978-1-955169-13-4

Previous Edition Copyright © 2018 by J F Rogers

Editing by Brilliant Cut Editing
Cover design by 100 Covers

Published by Noblebright Publishing
Sanford, ME
www.noblebrightpublishing.com

For I can do everything through Christ, who gives me strength.

— PHILIPPIANS 4:13

CHAPTER ONE

Pepin held the boulder to his chest and, with a grunt, focused on his mark. If only he could wipe the sweat from his eyes and the fear from his heart. He forced himself to breathe despite the weight against his chest. Still, his face must be as red as his hair. His entire life so far had culminated to this moment, the final test of strength required of every male pech.

He only had to beat Frode.

Pepin adjusted his grip and tried to ignore the thousands of pech filling the stands in the massive underground arena—and the unnatural hush that had come over them. He'd tossed boulders farther than Frode in practice runs. But Frode had just broken a record for himself. And now, beating him required breaking a personal record as well.

Torsten, or whichever god is listening, please don't let me lose.

Pepin bent his knees and roared as he ran to the line,

pushed through his legs to his arms, and sent the stone soaring. He held his breath as the rock arched high.

Further. Just a little further.

He didn't need to win by much. He just couldn't lose. If he lost, he'd be the lowliest of the low.

The boulder began its descent. His stomach twisted as he calculated its fall. The stone dropped, and his shoulders dropped too. Its thud in the sand echoing in the arena, it landed about twenty centimeters behind Frode's.

He'd come in last.

Last, last, last, the reverberations seemed to accuse.

Booing followed the echo as pech sprang from their seats. Above all else, other than dishonoring their gods, Pech abhorred those they considered weak. Hurled food splattered him. An egg smacked his temple. The shell cut his skin. Yolk or blood dripped down his cheek. Probably both.

Last place. The class loser.

The graduates gathered. Red hair that escaped from braids stuck to their faces. Tunics clung to their chests. Stink clogged the airway.

Frode's pitying look hurt more than the jeers. His friend would stay away from him now. No one associated with the class loser.

Magnar took center place as the victor, and the class swarmed him. Pepin allowed Magnar to climb upon his shoulders. They paraded before the assembly who cheered for Magnar.

Then the victor leapt from Pepin's shoulders, and his triumphant roar made the crowd scream. The competitors lined up, him in the lead and Pepin in back, behind Frode. Their teacher adorned Magnar with a stone necklace—twelve stones looped together to signify unending strength for each of the twelve moons. Then he came to Pepin and tied a rope around his neck for Frode to pull.

Pepin scanned the arena for his family. But couldn't spot them in this crowd. All the pech had long red hair, both male and female. Other than the elderly. Didn't matter. He'd never see them again. They'd slip away to avoid witnessing his disgrace and to declare his dismissal from their family.

Made sense. Still, their rejection bored out his core and filled the emptiness with acid each time he thought about it. Today, he was no longer a fledgling in need of family, yet he felt like an orphan.

Would no one stand on his behalf?

The class paraded through the marketplace. Everywhere, Magnar received applause, while Pepin was heckled, a target for food.

CHAPTER TWO

Pepin scurried around Annar's laboratory, as jittery as if he'd drank an entire cask of mung juice. Lantern light—it and the lit fireplace providing the only light in the underground room—flickered on the rock walls, mirroring his jitters. His kind teacher took Pepin in after his family abandoned him. But Annar had been growing impatient over the past year. If Pepin ruined one more amulet, Annar would dismiss him. Then where would Pepin go? He'd be forced to leave the Tower's safety, expelled into the world that belonged to the gachen.

He pulled the mold from the fire, exhaling as the clay smoked. It looked perfect, exactly as he'd seen Annar's. Once it cooled enough, he'd emboss it with the element markings for travel between the megaliths. He set his internal clock to emboss it at precisely the right time. This time, he would not fail. He'd make his teacher proud and keep his place, even his lowly place, in the Tower.

He cleared the stone-slab counter, replacing the tools as Annar had taught him.

"What have you done?" shouted Annar.

Pepin flinched and nearly fell. Catching himself on the counter, he hit a chisel on the edge and sent it flying. The chisel crashed into the pots and pans he'd haphazardly stacked on the tallest ledge, toppling them.

One spun before coming to a stop. When the clatter stilled, he faced his teacher.

Annar smacked himself and dragged his hand across his cheek, letting out an exasperated groan. "Pepin, Pepin, Pepin." He shook his head, then picked up the mold. "Are you incapable of the simplest task?"

"It's not ready to emboss, master."

"Nor will it ever be." He slumped to the carved lime-stone seat by the table. "What am I going to do with you? I've been training you for more than a year. The inter-realm transport stone is the most basic amulet. I learned to make one in a month. You still can't get it right. You've used the wrong ratios." He held a stone he'd made last week. "See this?"

Holding his breath, Pepin moved closer.

"What differences do you notice?"

"Your amulet is darker, but once it dries—"

"It will lighten, Pepin. *Lighten.* Do you see? You're proving my point. You should have realized your ratios were off before putting it into the kiln. Do you have any idea how much you cost me in wasted materials?"

He shuffled his feet. Of course, he knew. Annar reminded him more and more these days.

Annar rubbed between his fuzzy brows. Still, they drooped over sorrowful eyes. "I'd hoped things would turn out differently. I've done what I can to keep the king's council from banishing you. But I can no longer justify keeping you on as an apprentice."

His heart thudding, Pepin clasped his hands behind his back. "But where will I go, master?"

"I don't know. I'll give you three days to figure it out. Three days." Annar held up three stubby fingers as if he needed to ensure Pepin could comprehend the number. "Then you must leave."

CHAPTER THREE

Pepin flopped from side to side on his pallet that night. His blanket twisted around his restless legs.

Three days. Three days. Three days.

Less than three days. The moment Annar uttered those words, time started ticking down.

Where would he go? What would he do? He'd never left the Tower. Long ago, before gachen arrived, pech were the only race in Ariboslia. They had nothing to fear. Now, they had to invent stories about giants. Hundreds of years ago, they even built the Tower to keep up the ruse.

He'd never met a pech who'd ventured outside the Tower. Some traded between the Tower and Ceas Croi, yes. But he'd never met any. And it was dangerous work. There were rumors of gachen who drank blood. Blood!

Pepin shuddered.

He would never survive out there.

But, in less than three days, he'd have no choice. Where

would he go? Would the gachen find him? The blood-drinking ones?

A brilliant light blazed into the cramped room birthed from solid rock.

What in Torsten's blessed mines?

Holding a hand to protect his eyes, he scrambled up and pushed himself into the corner as far from the light as possible. The brightness flickered, dimming, brightening, then dimming again as if attempting to adjust itself for him.

"Do not be afraid."

When the light dimmed enough for him to look at the thing, he peered through his spread fingers. It had a body like none other. Tall, with long limbs and no facial hair. Covered by a dazzling white robe cinched at the waist with a golden rope.

He lowered his shaky hands, able to behold it unshielded now. "What are you?"

"I'm an angel sent by God."

"Torsten sent you? Or another god?"

"There is only one God. Torsten is a figment of your ancestors' imagination."

All thought vanished from Pepin's mind. After several hammer strikes, his brain resumed, and he picked away at his knowledge of Torsten and the minor gods. He'd followed all the rules, recited all the chants to the appropriate god in the proper hour and season. Well, mostly. He'd been better at that than amulet making... or anything else. Still, his people rejected him. Still, he'd failed in almost every way possible. Was that because... was it possible that...

There was no Torsten?

He flinched, cowering to protect himself. Torsten's sword was sure to cut him down for such thoughts.

Was there another, more powerful God? "Who is *your* God?"

"He is the Creator of all things. The great I Am. The Beginning and the End. The Author and the Finisher."

Tears slid into Pepin's beard. He didn't understand why, but these names pushed unfathomable emotions within him. "I'm not worthy of notice from such a God."

"You are wrong. God has seen your affliction and has compassion for you. He has given me this message: You are to create an inter-realm transport amulet of limestone, turquoise, and malachite. The face must bear this symbol." A piece of parchment drifted to the stone floor at the angel's feet. Markings burned the paper, and a symbol took shape. "When it is complete, give it to the elders of Notirr. It will require a jewel found in the Sea of Firinne."

Pepin's stomach liquefied like stone in a blazing oven. "I can't even make a traditional inter-realm amulet." He gripped his head as if to keep his brain from melting, too. "How can I make one with these materials?"

"All things are possible with God," the angel said. "You must believe."

"But—"

The angel disappeared.

Pepin lit his bedside lantern. He reached for the parchment, half-expecting it to burn him, but found it cool. He studied the symbol, a star with six points and strange etchings between and at their tips. An indentation dipped the center inward, presumably where the jewel belonged.

He'd failed countless attempts at the most basic amulet. And he'd never worked with turquoise. Did Annar even have any?

In less than three days, Annar would force him to leave. At least he now had somewhere to go—Notirr.

But how would he make the amulet?

CHAPTER FOUR

Too anxious to sleep, Pepin paced Annar's caverns. Something burned within him as if his soul had caught fire.

He needed to make the amulet. And he needed to make it now.

First, he needed limestone.

No problem. Annar had plenty. And malachite had to be around here somewhere. Pepin rummaged through Annar's storage, digging behind sacks of clay, various salts, and powdered granite until he found it. Turquoise though? *Please, please, please, let there be turquoise.*

He couldn't find it. His heart sank as tied to a millstone.

"What are you doing?" Annar stood in the doorway, wearing his nightcap and gown and rubbing his eyes.

"Um. I'm—"

"Pepin." Annar tapped a foot, his tone low and threatening.

Better to be honest. Pepin only had three days left,

anyway. Not even. What else could he lose? "Do you have any turquoise?"

"What in Torsten's name do you need turquoise for?"

"Um, I, uh..." He clutched his hands behind his back and scuffled his feet.

Annar crossed his arms.

"I need it for an amulet."

"What amulet are you attempting to make that requires something as rare as turquoise?"

"Uh, um, an inter-realm travel amulet."

"I knew you were slow, but this is beyond—" Annar's furry eyebrows jumped around his forehead, and his reddish complexion took on a deeper hue. "Such a simple amulet doesn't require turquoise. You're not even capable of making one with basic materials."

Something deep within Pepin surfaced, keeping him calm. A newfound strength. "An angel told me to make an inter-realm transport amulet with limestone, turquoise, and malachite bearing this mark."

When Pepin pulled the parchment from his pocket and unfolded it, Annar snatched the template and studied it. "Where did you get this?"

"I told you. An angel gave it to me."

"An angel you say." Annar tugged his beard.

"Have you heard of angels?"

"My grandfather talked about them when I was a fledgling." Annar handed back the parchment. "Better get to work. I'll fetch the turquoise."

CHAPTER FIVE

Each day, as Pepin worked, he grew in anticipation and hope. It was different this time. He wasn't nervous. And he didn't need a formula to follow. He *knew* what to do. On instinct. And Annar gave him complete access to his supplies.

Before the third day ended, he completed the amulet—a stunning piece of work.

"I must confess." Annar swiped the counter with a rag, the polished stone smooth beneath his strokes. "I would have bet my last coin that you weren't up to the task. It's a rare beauty."

Buoyed, Pepin rocked back on his toes. If only he could hold on to this feeling of accomplishment forever. "I couldn't have done it without you."

"That's true." Annar laughed, then dropped the rag on the counter. "Perhaps I was a bit harsh."

"No, you've given me many chances. I've never been a good student."

"It's an honor to see you complete this great task—and in a mere three days. Such zeal and dedication, you've scarcely slept. I believe an angel did visit you. The God he represents must be real as well. So, I will seek this God for myself. But now you must go, deliver the amulet to Notirr as directed. But know this—you have a home here."

"Master!" Pepin rushed into Annar's arms and hugged him. Something only fledglings did with their mothers. Oops. Heat tingling up his neck, Pepin backed away. "My apologies, I—"

"No need to apologize. I see you appreciate my offer and take your response as a yes."

"Yes! Oh yes. Thank you, master."

"Well then, pack your things, and I'll see you off."

With his meager belongings in a satchel, he waited for Annar at the entrance to his dwelling.

"Don't forget, stone exists everywhere outside these walls. You will be able to sense them. Use them to aid you as shelter or weapons as you need. And here." Annar pulled a rock casket from a shelf, clattered off the lid, and peeled away a red cloth. A dagger. "This belonged to my grandfather. Since you're on a quest of which he'd approve, I want you to wield it."

Pepin accepted it with a brief dip of his head. "I am most honored."

"Come, then. Let us be off."

Annar led him through the marketplace. Though the tower offered miles of headroom in the center, it still felt cramped, stifling. Booths packed together with little room for wares, and their buyers cared naught for those trying to pass through. Pepin stood shoulder height to the menfolk and just shy of meeting most of the womenfolk eye-to-eye. So, he was accustomed to taking shoulder checks and chest bumps pushing him out of the way.

Sharp, disapproving looks pierced him from those who noticed him. No wonder he rarely ventured from Annar's chamber.

Pepin rounded a corner and bumped into Magnar.

CHAPTER SIX

Pepin hopped back a step, recovering his balance on a man sitting outside the Wurzelgemüse Suppe stand, making him spill his soup. Several onlookers snickered while the woman running the booth clicked her tongue.

The man growled, barely glancing over his shoulder. "Watch yourself, klumpen."

Pepin jerked away while avoiding Magnar like the two-headed uilebheist.

"If it isn't the runt." Magnar's lips curved into a wicked smile. "What crevice did you drag yourself out of?"

"I, uh..." Pepin looked to Annar for support.

"Hail, Magnar." Annar slapped Magnar on his back hard enough to make him pitch forward. "I understand you're training to be a commander in the royal guard. Congratulations, lad."

Pepin stifled his urge to laugh. Only Annar could be so complimentary and yet so condescending at the same time.

"Much obliged, Sir Annar." Magnar stepped in front of

Annar and, hands on his hips, faced Pepin. "I trust you intend to crawl back into whatever you crawled out of."

What audacity and in Annar's presence? Magnar must truly think himself special.

A desire—no, a *need*—to show Magnar up made Pepin stand taller. Even at his full height, he couldn't come eye-to-eye. Still, he met Magnar's stare. "I'm leaving the Tower."

Gasps surrounded Pepin as those within earshot stopped what they were doing and gathered around. The crowd seemed to confuse Magnar. His facade cracked, but only for a moment. He poked Pepin's chest. "How will a runt survive outside these walls? You'll be food for the gachen."

"I don't think they eat pech." But what of the blood drinkers?

"They eat runts like you." Magnar's fat finger poked Pepin again and hit the amulet. He jerked his hand back, his gaze narrowing "What was that?"

"It's no–nothing."

A devilish grin split Magnar's still scraggly beard. "Are you sneaking an amulet outside these walls? I trust you have the proper permissions."

"Simmer down, cadet." Annar crossed his arms. "You don't have authority to accuse anyone."

"I do." Ingharr came up behind Pepin, grabbed the stone, and pulled, breaking the leather cord.

Pepin rubbed his stinging neck.

"What kind of amulet is this?" Ingharr scraped at its edges. "What are these markings?"

"An angel told me how to make it," Pepin said.

More gasps echoed around them.

At the fear flaring in Annar's eyes, Pepin's heartbeat skittered. He should have kept silent!

"A what?" Ingharr's eyes bulged. "Did you say, angel?"

If only Pepin could deny the words. But he dared not deny the truth now. While he feared Ingharr and many others who wished him harm, he feared God more.

"The only time I've heard mention of angels is in reference to a god. A god who opposes Torsten and all our other gods." Ingharr stepped so close, Pepin smelled his breath. He must've just eaten mushroom stew. "Is that who you claim to have spoken to? A representative of an opposing god?"

That inexplicable courage again girded him. "I'm referring to a messenger of the One True God."

A woman fainted. Pech attended to her while keeping an eye on him. The crowd grew.

Purple splotches mottled Ingharr's face. Spittle landed on Pepin as Ingharr tried to form words. "Y–you—" He stepped back and pointed to the ground. "Kneel in homage to your god, Torsten, now, while he allows you to continue to breathe."

A tiny voice in Pepin's mind urged him to kneel. But the boldness empowering him hadn't left. "I will kneel to no other god, but the One True God."

Ingharr's whole body shook. His fists and teeth clenched. If he'd been a kettle, the top would've blown off already. "T–take–take him to the uilebheist."

When Magnar grabbed Pepin's arm and pulled, Annar

grasped Pepin's other arm, rooting him. "I don't care if you are head of the king's council, Ingharr. You can't kill the lad without a trial, without the king's explicit permission."

"You saw it." Ingharr waved to the crowd. "You saw his refusal to kneel for Torsten and his blatant allegiance to an opposing god. Am I right?"

Every head in Pepin's line of sight nodded. Grunts and words of approval came from those heads and more. They had just sentenced him with the death penalty.

CHAPTER SEVEN

Pepin landed on the cold, unforgiving stone. He rolled to soften the blow. Pain shot up from his right knee. The grate above him slid back into place with a grinding sure to rouse the beast. If the noise from his fall hadn't.

He had to get up before he became the uilebheist's meal.

He peeled himself from the ground and wiped the blood and scraped skin from his hands. A tear in his pants exposed his bloodied knee. He couldn't do anything about it now.

He searched the darkness. The beast might come from any direction, and Pepin was unarmed. A dim glow filtered through the overhead grate, the only light source. No one watched from there. The few witnesses allowed probably sat in the dark on the sidelines, behind the safety of steel beams. Assuming the rumors were true.

First, he'd better get out of the spotlight. But in which direction? He inched into the dim recesses, then stopped to listen. Was that breathing? Was it his own, the crowd's, or the uilebheist's?

If only he had the Annar's dagger. Not that it would be much help against an uilebheist.

Breathing. Now, he heard breathing. And he hadn't moved. So, it wasn't the crowd, but the beast.

A thud echoed. Another. And another. Footsteps clambered his way. He backed away, careful not to make a sound. A growl accompanied the thuds. A silhouette solidified. A scaly head thrust into the light and flinched, shying at the glare. It opened its mouth, uncurled its slithery tongue, and unleashed its roar. A putrid wind circled the cavern.

Another head emerged from the darkness. And another. The red hairs covering Pepin's arms stood on end. How many heads did this beast have?

The other heads reacted to the light. The creature wasn't too sharp. A webbed foot slapped the ground. Its tail swished, slicing the air, its tip resembling the flippers their books depicted of selkie in their seal form. Did this creature belong in the sea?

A head passed through the light, its nostrils flaring as if catching the scent of prey. Pepin scrambled backward. His back connected with a wall and slid along it, yet the beast continued stalking him.

God, did You reveal Yourself to me just to kill me now?

But why ask the obvious? No one had ever survived the uilebheist.

Pepin dug into his pockets. He wasn't sure why. They'd checked him before throwing him down here. And nothing short of a miracle would help him. But still, he felt around. His right hand touched something hard and round. A pebble?

He pulled it free, fumbling to feel what he couldn't see. But it was small. No way could he slay the beast with a pebble. But, if he managed to survive, they had to set him free. That was the law.

And his only hope.

Throw it.

What was that? Had someone spoken? He almost spun around. But he hadn't heard it aloud, but in his head.

Yet the thought hadn't come from him.

The middle head roared, sending another noxious breeze.

Now!

He wound his arm back and hurled the pebble with every ounce of his strength.

The uilebheist choked and reared, nearly colliding with the grate above. A horrid gurgling emanated from its throat as the other two heads tried moving in different directions. The monster charged him.

He ran at the uilebheist, sliding under its legs to the other side.

The creature moved too fast to stop and crashed into the wall. It rose and staggered. Foam dripped from the middle head. Its eyes rolled back in its head, and it went limp. The remaining heads watched one another, eyes wide, as the beast fell to the ground. They gnashed their teeth while it tried to stand, then fell back to the floor. The body and remaining heads convulsed. Then they let out another breath and... stilled.

He dropped to his knees, panting, barely aware of the throbbing pain from his bloodied knee. Tears coursed through his beard as he praised God.

With God's help, he, the lowly Pepin, had defeated the uilebheist.

CHAPTER EIGHT

After two weeks of travel, Pepin grew to appreciate the world outside the Tower of Galore. He breathed in fresh air, not laced with thick woodsmoke and cloying mustiness of middle earth, glad God had proven He was with Pepin by helping him defeat the uilebheist before this quest.

Only God could have slipped that glemmestein into his pocket. And only God knew glemmestein is poisonous to sea creatures ... or that an uilebheist *was* a sea creature.

Pepin peeked out from behind a tree and surveyed the tall, slim man at Notirr's gate. He'd seen gachen in his travels. But he shied away. He took a deep breath, swallowing down the bile of Magnar saying they ate runts like Pepin.

He didn't *look* like he drank blood.

You are with me, God. I trust You.

Pepin stepped out from behind the tree. He puffed out his chest and approached the gate.

The gachen's mouth dropped as Pepin advanced.

"Eh hem." Pepin cleared his throat. "Where might I find an elder?"

"Are ye?" The man leaned closer, blinked, and squinted. "Are ye a pech?"

"I am." Pepin lifted his chin, proud of his heritage despite its flaws.

"Pardon me." The man straightened. "It's just… I've heard tell of pech, but I've never seen one. Come to think of it, I've never seen a giant or a selkie either. What brings ye to Notirr?"

"I've an important message for the elders."

"Have ye any weapons?"

Pepin fingered the dagger's hilt at his waist. He hesitated, then extracted it from the sheath. "Just a dagger."

The man took the weapon, ran a finger along the blade, and whistled. "'Tis a beauty. I've never seen such fine craftsmanship."

Annar's kindness warmed Pepin anew. "It was a gift."

"I'll be sure to return it." The man opened the gate. "You there, Cahal."

A neckless mountain of a man with dark hair and piercing eyes approached. Cuts marked his face and arms. Bandages covered his shoulder. What happened to him?

Pepin held his breath. His gaze continued upward and upward as the giant approached. But giants weren't real. The pech invented them and spread rumors to keep the gachen away.

Was this man a giant? Did giants eat pech?

Pepin scrambled a few steps back.

"Cahal, this man… er—"

"Pepin."

"Aye. Pepin is requesting an audience with an elder. Would you take him to Quin?"

Without speaking, Cahal motioned for Pepin to follow, casting a long shadow Pepin tried to avoid as he ran to keep up through windy paths of homes in hills. Cahal stopped and knocked on a door.

When the door opened, a much smaller man, more the size of the one at the gate, smiled from within. "Cahal, I see you've brought me a visitor. To what might I owe this pleasure?"

"He asked to see an elder."

"I have a gift for you," Pepin said.

"Well, let's have a look, shall we?" The elder who must be Quin opened the door for Pepin to step through.

Cahal spun on his heels and tromped along the path.

"Cahal is a man of few words and an intimidating sight, but he is a kind soul," Quin said. "I hope you don't mind. The clan elders are here."

"My apologies." Pepin bowed. "I don't mean to intrude."

"No worries, my friend. 'Tis no imposition. Join us."

Light streamed through the only window. Seven people —some huddling together on a wooden couch, others sitting in chairs they must've brought in for this gathering—said hello or waved.

Pepin bowed and thumped his chest twice to greet them in return.

A gray-haired man occupied a rocker next to the

window. Something was wrong with his eyes. They had no color. Just gray where the color should be.

A woman sat with a fledgling girl. If gachen aged like the pech, the girl had probably lived fifteen years. A bit old to sit hugging what must be her mother. The girl stared through strands of blond hair, her eyes puffy and wet. Her mother stroked the girl's hair and kissed her head.

"Please, have a seat." Quin pulled another wooden chair into the room.

Pepin eased himself up on the seat, his legs dangled like a fledgling.

"Welcome, Pepin," the man with colorless eyes said. "I'm called Sully."

Eh? Pepin jolted. How did he know Pepin's name? Neither he nor Cahal had spoken it. Pepin swallowed. Perhaps he'd made a mistake walking so boldly into a gachen village.

Quin handed Pepin a drink and sat in a chair across from him. "What is this gift you speak of? It must be important. Pech tend to keep to themselves. I've only met one once."

He'd met a pech? Head cocked, Pepin almost asked how and when. But no. He'd come to deliver his gift, nothing more, nothing less. He extracted the stone from inside his shirt. Annar had strung it with a new cord. Neither Pepin nor Annar knew its capabilities. But it would do whatever God intended it to do. Not that it mattered. God wanted it made and delivered, and Pepin would complete the task.

"Is this the amulet?" Quin took the stone and looked to Sully.

"Aye." Sully nodded. "'Tis Drochaid."

Drochaid?

"This will allow travel between realms?" Quin asked.

Few were allowed to test amulets within the Tower. Annar hadn't had time, nor would he have been able to convince the king to let Pepin leave with it if he had. "It should, but I haven't tested it yet. Nor have I named it."

"God named it. And I'm sure it will work. We'll need Pepin to show us how to use it to save Cataleen from Aodan." Sully nodded toward the girl.

Did they intend to send her to the human realm? Pepin swallowed the lump forming in his throat. He only knew how to open the megalith with an amulet in theory, not practice. But God had gotten him this far. God would see him all the way through—wouldn't He?

"Well." Quin leaned back. "I don't know why these things still amaze me. Pepin, you must be an important man of God for Him to use you like this."

Man of God. That sounded good. He relaxed. He was among believers. Their race no longer mattered. They were kin.

"If Sully is correct"—Quin gave Sully a knowing smile —"and, as a prophet who speaks for God, he usually is, we need your help. Will you join us?"

A month ago, Pepin was an embarrassment to his people. A runt. Incapable of creating a simple amulet. Today, he was a new person.

With God, he'd created an amulet with abilities yet to

be discovered. With God, he'd defeated the uilebheist and claimed his freedom.

With God, he could do anything.

He looked at the hopeful faces awaiting his response. "I'd be honored."

SHAMELESS REQUEST FOR
REVIEWS

Authors need reviews! They help books get noticed, and I love to know what readers think of my stories. So, if you enjoyed this book, please consider leaving a review where you purchased this book, Goodreads, BookBub... anywhere you think a review might be helpful. I'm forever grateful!

You are loved,

JF Rogers

PROLOGUE

In the foothills of rural Maine

Under the cover of night, hidden in the rickety tree house in the backyard, De'Mere waited, watching. The fort offered all he needed, privacy and the perfect vantage point. He peered into the upper right-hand window of the old farmhouse across the lawn. The alarm clock's glow illuminated Fallon's room in an alien-like green. Only her feet at the edge of the bed lay within view. Their stirring told him she was having a nightmare—again.

He slumped against the rough, far wall and peeked at the sky through wide gaps in the roof. The sun would soon rise. He'd retreat to the wood to rest until it was time to return. Then his real work would begin.

"De'Mere," a thunderous, yet oddly melodic voice called.

De'Mere bristled as chills coursed down his spine. He jumped to his feet, bumped his head on the low ceiling, and dropped to his knees to peer out the windows.

"De'Mere." The voice seemed to float in midair right in front of his face. He fell back, away from the window, and reached out, groping air with his right hand for something solid, perturbed that his otherwise keen eyesight failed him at this crucial time. This must be how a blind man might feel, sneaked up on, spoken to without warning.

"Your time has nearly come." The voice stimulated a fresh course of chills surging throughout his being. It commanded attention, and for a creature such as himself, invoked fear. Its very presence filled the confined space. "Do you remember what to do?"

De'Mere continued his search for clues as to its whereabouts. It seemed to be everywhere. An internal struggle raged between his desperate desire to find the owner of the voice and his equal need to shy away. He craved a glimpse, if only to determine where to draw near or in which direction to run.

"Do you know what to do?"

"Yes," he answered in a hurried, hushed tone, afraid to elicit an unwelcome audience, which didn't appear to concern the disembodied voice. But then, perhaps it wasn't audible to anyone but him. "But how do I make sure she's there?"

"Just do your part. Tonight."

The air no longer squeezed De'Mere like an invisible vise. The unearthly being was gone. He took a deep breath, savoring his solitude. But the hollow cavity within him widened. If only he could fill the void.

He returned his attention to Fallon's bedroom. The sheet lay flat. She must have risen while he'd been distracted. Had she overheard their voices and come outside? He peered down the hole in the floor. The ladder was bare. Careful to avoid the squeaky planks, he crossed to the window closest to the house. He dared stick his head out enough to search the darkness below, hoping it wasn't a mistake. He'd come too far to risk exposure now.

The night was still. As if all living things had been frightened away. The breeze dared not even rustle a leaf. He ducked back inside and searched the path to the house. Still nothing. Crickets chirping in the distance offered the only sign of life.

He glanced back at the house. Light filled the bathroom window. A shadow moved beyond the drawn shade. Releasing the air he'd been holding, he laughed softly at his paranoia. He was much too far away for a mere human to hear.

"Tonight," De'Mere whispered, the word lingering in the air.

After all these years, the time had come. His watching and waiting would soon be over. He'd play his part. The trick would be getting Fallon to play hers.

He descended from the tree house by dropping out the trapdoor. After landing with a soft thud on the unkempt lawn, he ran on all fours for the cover of the tree line.

CHAPTER ONE

The sun's unnatural glow blinded me. Tears coursed down my face as I struggled to take in my surroundings. With each blink, a woman with long, blonde hair dappled in gold sparkles grew clearer. She sat motionless on the sand, watching the ocean waves. I couldn't see her face, but imagined she awaited her long-lost love from beneath the watery depths. A breeze swept across the shore, swirling the white dress around her delicate frame as tresses danced about her face.

The wind carried my name, long and silvery sweet, "Fallon...Faaaaallon."

A shiver ran through me. Was she calling me? Did I know her? A dream. This had to be a dream.

Something about her was familiar. Overcome with an unsettling compulsion to be near her, I walked in her direction. But the woman remained the same distance away. I paused, blinking to ensure I wasn't seeing things, and then quickened my pace. Still, I made no ground. I ran. Again, no progress. Frustrated, I stopped.

The woman slowly turned to face me.

Shadows overtook the landscape as storm clouds choked the sun. Neither of us moved, yet the woman was closer. The entire scene was now mere feet before me, as if I'd somehow crossed a considerable distance. In one fluid motion, her hair transformed from blonde to black. As the serene face mutated, curiosity morphed into disquiet in the pit of my stomach. I gasped. I recognized deep purple eyes unobscured by thick lenses. The pasty, oblong face minus the acne. Me—only beautiful. With an eerie lack of emotion, the doppelganger's face tilted sideways. My stomach tightened with each passing second that those dead eyes watched me until I nearly doubled over in pain.

Without warning, its mouth widened. Baring sharp, menacing fangs, it lunged at me.

Just before it reached me, my body spasms jerked me awake, as if I'd fallen from the ceiling onto the bed. Entangled in my sheets, I fought to free myself. As reality set in, my thudding heart descended to its natural rhythm. I let out a slow, even breath and glanced at the alarm clock's glowing digits, squinting to make sense of them—3:56 a.m.

Something was off. The air sizzled, as though an unseen electrical current ran through it. I felt a presence. Within reach, yet so far away. The more I grasped for what it might be, the more it evaded me. Something lurked in the shadows. I was certain of it.

I put on my glasses and fumbled with the bedside lamp, knocking it to the floor. I stilled, holding my breath, waiting for whatever remained hidden in the darkness to jump me.

Nothing moved.

Rather than drape my feet over the bed and give any monster lurking there a chance to grab my ankles, I stood and jumped far out of reach. I landed on the creaky oak floorboards and hurried to the bathroom to flip on the light switch before something could sneak up behind me in the dark. I shook my head at myself. If Stacy could see me now, avoiding the boogeyman under my bed, she'd tease me mercilessly.

After splashing cold water on my face, hoping to wash

away the dream, I put on my glasses and eyed my reflection. My face, littered with acne no astringent could clear up, scowled back. My purple eyes, magnified in the thick frames, glared. If only I were truly as beautiful as in the dream, for the brief moment before it changed. The fanged creature came to mind. I shuddered, grabbed a towel, and dried off.

I lumbered back to my room and picked up the lamp. The light erased all but a few shadows, which I took time to investigate personally.

I eyed everything with extreme scrutiny, even the flowery, yellowed wallpaper, peeling in places, certain a chameleonlike creature could hide itself there. But nothing bulged. I flung back the once beautiful pink bedding that now looked like something from a hamster cage. Ratty. But the sheet lay flat.

Other than the wear and tear, my room hadn't changed in ten years. Not since Bumpah died. After that, Fiona stopped taking care of...well...everything. She threw money at me every once in a while so Stacy's mom could take me clothes shopping or to doctor appointments. Other than that, she never gave me anything, not even on my birthday.

My birthday. Today. My seventeenth birthday. The first day of summer. I flopped on my bed, grateful school was over until fall, but I couldn't face another birthday without Bumpah. No, I wouldn't allow myself to think about it.

I glanced at the book overhanging my bedside table and snatched it up, eager to escape to the world within its pages. My bookmark fell out, and I grumbled as I found my spot.

Reading about other worlds usually calmed me, but the words refused to sink in. Instead, Bumpah kept popping into my mind. The hollow within me widened. I needed him to pull me out of my funk. I could almost hear him joking, comparing my moods to the New England weather. "If you don't like it, wait a minute," he'd say. Then he'd sing and dance around like a goof. Inevitably, a smile returned to my face.

I needed Bumpah to calm the storm, to make my birthday special. All I had was Fiona, and she couldn't care less. Instead of loving me as her granddaughter, she treated me like an annoying customer lingering past closing. Or worse.

The whirlwind of darkness engulfed me. Tears slipped down my cheeks. I pulled my knees up and wrapped my arms around myself. My hands ran over the scars, reminding me I could, once more, deal with the pain. But no, I'd promised Stacy, the only one who knew my secret and still cared about me, for whatever reason. Perhaps I should try talking to her God.

"God, if you're really there, I don't know why you'd listen to me, but Stacy keeps asking me to, so here goes. God, I don't know what to do. I'm so angry. All the time. I can't help it. My grandmother hates me. I don't have any family. I'm all al—" My voice cracked and tears poured. "I don't want to be this way." I slammed my fist against the pillow. "Why'd you take my family away? You never even gave me a chance. Are you even there? Do you even care?"

Nothing. No response. I wiped my eyes and returned to my book with renewed focus, determined to escape reality. At least I could tell Stacy I'd tried. If her God was real, He must hate me.

When the sun's rays streamed into the room, overheating me, I found the book open with the pages bent under my face. I folded them back in place, checked for drool, and returned it to my bedside, hoping the librarian wouldn't notice or care. Then I threw on a crumpled pair of jeans and a black T-shirt before heading to the kitchen.

I paused at the top of the stairs and took a deep breath. As I stared at the worn treads, I prepped myself for the off chance that I might come in contact with Fiona. "It's just another day like any other. Don't expect anything from her. It doesn't matter that it's your birthday." No matter what, this year, I would not get my hopes up.

I shuffled downstairs then through the dining room to the kitchen. Fiona's immense plate collection in the hutch rattled in my wake.

Fiona sat at the kitchen table, eating a late breakfast. She dropped her head, shaggy gray hair falling around her face as she wiped her eyes, and shoved a postcard into the pocket of the drab brown sweater she always wore—even in this summer heat.

I almost turned and left, but I needed coffee. Sighing, I plodded to the coffee maker, eyeing the cracked black-and-white checkered tile as I went. My tangled mass of black hair dangled in my face, shielding me from view.

Fiona slurped her coffee. "Look who decided to grace us with her presence."

I wanted to ask if "us" included her many personalities. I bit my tongue. Instead, I grunted something resembling "morning."

I hoped she'd leave it at that. Nothing good came from conversation with Fiona. The more I allowed the woman to voice her opinion, the greater the chance I'd run away in tears. She was a guilt-trip ninja, striking when I least expected.

"I have something for you."

A warning thumped in my chest. I continued to stir the cream and sugar in my coffee, too much of each. I turned to face her. "What is it?"

"Oh, for Pete's sake, stop gawking and come here, Fallon."

I peered with extreme caution into her outstretched palm.

"Well, take it." She shook the object clasped in her meaty fingers.

Like a game of Operation, I snatched it and removed my hand as fast as possible as if to avoid the buzzing sound. I then backed to a more comfortable distance.

A necklace. I sucked in my breath. The pendent seemed ancient. A heavy circle made from some type of gray stone attached to a leather cord. Seven cone shapes pointed from a circular indent in the center, giving it the shape of a star or a sun. Strange marks, like hieroglyphics, each unique, etched deep between the points.

It had been so long since I'd received a gift I didn't know how to respond. "What is it?"

"Not quite sure. It belonged to your mother."

"My mother?" The amulet fell, the cord caught around my finger. I pulled it to safety and let out a heavy breath. My mother. I couldn't remember the last time she was mentioned in this house.

Fiona's steel-blue eyes lost their sharpness for a nanosecond. "Yes." Then with a quick shake of her head, adding more volume to her frizzy hair, she stood and brought her dishes to the sink. "Well, enough of that."

"No." My mother's ghost had been summoned. I couldn't let it float away.

Fiona stuck out her jaw and glared at me with dead, unblinking eyes. My stomach jumped into my throat. I had ventured into dangerous territory, but I might never have another chance to find out about my mother. I'd searched this house from top to bottom for pictures—any insight into my parents—only to be denied. I tried softening my tone. "I mean...did my mother give this to you?"

Fiona dropped her gaze and returned to the sink. "No. She didn't."

"Well, who then? You've been holding on to it all these years? Why'd you give it to me now?"

Fiona placed her hands on her disproportionately large hips, lowered her head, and sighed. She remained like that, as though worn out from fighting down whatever humanity remained entombed within her otherwise heartless carcass.

After a few eons, she faced me. "Fallon, I really didn't know your mother well. This was given to Nathaniel after her..." She paused as if searching for the appropriate word. "...disappearance. He was instructed to hold onto it until your seventeenth birthday then give it to you. He's not here, so I'm doing it."

"Someone gave it to Bumpah *after* my mother...? Who?"

"I don't know. I wasn't there. He never said."

"But *why?* Why give this to me now? What for?"

Fiona folded her arms across her chest. She leaned toward me. Her pear-shaped frame extended as her face scrunched in a scowl, forcing the peach fuzz to stick out on her upper lip.

"I was tempted to throw the stupid thing away. I'm only doing this for Nathaniel. I promised."

Was she for real? I knew she hated me, but this was a whole new level of heartlessness. To want to toss the one thing connecting me to my mother...that was cold. My eyebrow twitched as I tried to think how to respond. I opened my mouth, but words escaped me. Her unblinking eyes bulged in my direction. Words I'd been dying to say for years flew from my mouth. "You're not the only one who lost your family, ya know. I miss Bumpah too. It's not fair. I can't even remember my parents. And I'm...I'm..." I knew what I wanted to say but couldn't bring myself to do it.

"You're *what?*"

Her nasty tone loosed my tongue. "I'm stuck with *you!*"

"Don't try to bait me. Nathaniel would still be here if it weren't for you. He was too old to be chasing after a rambunctious kid. As for my son—let me just say—no parent should outlive her child. *You* miss people you never knew. I lost the only people I ever loved. And where's your mother? I don't know. Her casket is empty next to my son's. Is *that* fair?" She paused as though I might actually reply. "For all I know, she killed him."

Fiona's chest heaved as she gulped for air, her face red. Blotchy. I stood frozen. Though her words stung, they didn't send me crying as they once had. Instead, they fueled my anger. I wanted nothing more than to smack her across the face. I fought to keep my clenched fists by my side. "What about me? I'm your granddaughter, remember? You didn't lose *everyone*."

Fiona shoved her hands into her pockets. "Oh for Pete's sake, I don't have time for this nonsense. I have more important things to attend to. Not all of us sleep until noon." She trudged out of the kitchen, leaving dirty dishes in the sink.

Blown off again. Fiona didn't have anything to do but send herself postcards from her dead husband, add to her ridiculous plate collection, and resent being stuck with me.

I dropped my cup into the sink, chipping it, and adding to the pile.

Several fantasies flashed across my mind. Most involved Fiona spinning and falling after a swift blow from a frying pan. Hurtful words I wished I'd said resonated in my mind. I cursed myself for allowing her to suck me in. I should know better by now.

My mind returned to the amulet. My first tangible connection to my mother. I placed it around my neck. It fell heavy against by breastbone. Warmth radiated from the spot, comforting me as if a missing piece of my heart had returned. I held it up to study the markings once more. As my fingers traced the cone shapes, feeling the rough surface, it sparked, like static electricity in the dark. I jumped. The necklace slipped from my fingers and thudded against my chest. My heart skittered. I yanked the stone off and dropped it on the counter.

Want to read more?
Pick up Astray at jfrogers.com/books/astray/

One elf. One dragon.

One deadly curse threatening them all.

Samu would do anything to be bonded to a dragon, even serve a king he doesn't trust. But when a strange mist falls over his city and the humans massacre the elves, the last thing he wants is to come to the king's rescue.

Then the dragon eggs are threatened, and the Divide grows dark.

This was no ordinary curse.

Someone... or something... is staging an extinction-level attack against the elves and their dragons.

But Samu won't let that happen. He can't. He'll rescue the dragons or die trying.

***The Darkening Divide* is the action-packed prequel to *The Cursed Lands* Christian fantasy adventure. If you enjoy mixing up genres with elves and dragons in a steampunk world infested with humans, download *The Darkening Divide* today! You'll love this intro to J F Rogers's exciting new series.**

Download The Darkening Divide today at jfrogers.com

ABOUT THE AUTHOR

J. F. Rogers lives in Southern Maine with her husband, daughter, pets... and an imaginary friend or two. She has a degree in Behavioral Science and teaches a 5th and 6th grade Sunday School class. When she's not entertaining Tuki the Mega Mutt, her constant companion and greatest distraction, she's likely tap, tap, tapping away at her keyboard, praying the words will miraculously align just so. Above all, she's a believer in the One True God and can say with certainty—you are loved.

Connect with J F Rogers

www. jfrogers.com

THE CURSED LANDS TRILOGY

Book I - The King's Curse

A king with a God complex. A cursed people.

Can one girl save their doomed souls?

COMING IN SPRING 2023!

Book I - Astray

A mysterious amulet leads Fallon to everything she's ever wanted...and possibly her death.

Book II - Adrift

Fallon returns to Ariboslia to save lives...but the creatures she wants to save want her dead.

Book III: Aloft

Fallon and Morrigan face off for the ultimate battle ... in their minds.

Prequel - Alight

Three friends. Evil seeks to corrupt them. If they survive... what will it cost?

ACKNOWLEDGMENTS

I'm so grateful to God for inspiring me and giving me the means to write. And for giving me a supportive husband. My family is such a gift.

Special thanks to:

- My amazing editor, Deirdre Lockhart, Brilliant Cut Editing.
- 100Covers and the infinitely patient Phyllis Ngo.
- All those who requested Pepin's Tale in paperback. It's such a short story, I never would have done it without some prodding. I hope you appreciate having a copy on your shelf. You know who you are. :)

God continues to send the right help and encouragement at the right time. I am beyond blessed. Thank you! I love you all!

You are loved,
J F Rogers